# *Edel Wignell*

# V O I C E S

Cover and text illustrations
by
David Kennett.

JUNIOR
NOVELS

This book is dedicated to

*Georgia* and *Heath*

# Contents

# Antarctic Egg

It was a freezing day in May. The female emperor penguin laid her greenish-white egg on the Antarctic ice. Quickly she pushed it with her beak up and under a big flap of skin, which looked like an apron, below her belly.

Her mate, the male emperor penguin, was with her. They called to each other with their trumpeting voices.

Early next day, the female penguin rolled the egg onto the male's feet, and he manoeuvred it under his fatty fold. There it was secure and warm — like a baby in a thick blanket.

The penguins trumpeted to each other again; both knew it was time for the female to go. At the same time, hundreds of voices were raised; hundreds of penguin pairs were parting. The males would stay in the rookery to care for the eggs, while the females would seek food.

# Scientists

Two scientists, Greg and Karen, stood at the edge of the rookery, watching the birds during the egg-laying.

The day before, Greg and Karen had walked among the penguins, making a film of the egg-laying, and taping the penguin voices. The penguins had ignored them for they had seen humans before. Humans had walked among them and had done no harm, so the birds felt no fear.

'I wonder how the females feel about leaving their eggs?' mused Greg. He had not liked leaving his family — his wife Jan and their girls — to travel to Antarctica.

Karen guessed that Greg was thinking about his new baby son, whom he had not met. News of the birth had come by radio-telephone.

'We'll be home soon,' she said. 'Only four months till we leave.'

'Yes, I know. I really miss them, and wonder what our new baby is like,' said Greg. 'I'll send the girls a fax tonight.'

| | |
|---|---|
| DATE: | **16 August 1990** |
| FAX TO: | **Sue and Peta, 61 8 8234 1234** |
| FROM: | **Dad, Mawson Base, Antarctica** |
| No. OF PAGES: | **1** |
| SUBJECT: | **A fax to my darling daughters** |

*Dear Sue and Peta,*

*Today Karen and I watched the penguins laying their eggs. The female knows that her egg would freeze in a few moments, so she pushes it up under a flap of skin to keep it warm and safe.*

*I wonder — is Harry a noisy baby? Well, he couldn't be as noisy as the penguins! They were deafening today — all trumpeting at once! Each one knows its mate and recognises its special voice. The females have now gone feeding and left the males with the eggs.*

*A big hug for Harry and much love to you both,*

*DAD*

13

# Dance to Your Daddy

The baby cried; he kicked and waved his fists. His mother Jan lifted him up to her shoulder and patted his back while she walked around the kitchen singing:

*Dance to your daddy, my little laddie,*
*Dance to your daddy, my little lamb.*
*You shall have a fishy in a little dishy,*
*You shall have a fishy when the boat*
*comes in.*

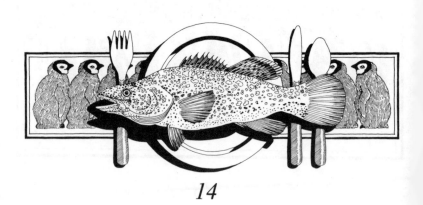

Harry burped, and his mother and two big sisters laughed.

'That's what he thinks of fish!' said Sue.

'He's too young for fish and chips,' said Peta.

'He'll make do with milk for a while yet,' said Jan. 'He won't go on to solid food till after Daddy comes home.'

'Wish Dad would hurry up.'

'Wish he hadn't gone to the Antarctic. What kind of presents can you bring from there? There are no shops. '

'Wish he'd gone to Hong Kong. He could bring me a radio . . . '

'Or a tape-recorder!'

'Greedy kids!' said Jan, undressing Harry. 'You shouldn't be thinking of presents. Just having Dad home will be marvellous, and specially wonderful for Harry. He doesn't even know he's got a father.'

She lifted Harry into the bath while Sue and Peta watched.

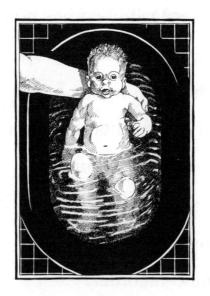

'Come on, girls. Talk to Harry.'

'He's too young to understand,' said Sue.

'Doesn't matter! It's good for him to hear your voices. He knows us by our voices as well as by our faces.'

'Funny face — funny voice,' said Jan, speaking in a squeaky voice and putting on a silly face.

Jan continued, 'If you two talk to him every day, he'll easily learn to speak. Tell him about his dad. While you talk, I'll take some photos.'

Peta began, 'Daddy's a scientist in Antarctica . . . '

# Penguin Chick

The female emperor penguin set off on her long, long trek with the other females from the rookery — away, away, away across the ice towards the open sea — a hundred kilometres away. A month ago, she and her mate had waddled all that distance up to the rookery, full of food, for it had been time to breed and lay.

At last the female penguin reached the sea. Immediately she dived, found a squid and ate it. Each day she hunted for fish and squid, and ate and ate, gorging herself.

As the weeks passed, she gathered a huge store of food within her body. It was like a larder — food ready to be used later by herself and her chick.

The females swam and fished together, their voices keeping them in touch. At the end of two months, it was time to return.

Heavy now, they set off — back, back, back across the icy waste. They pressed on, eager to return to their mates at the rookery. Perhaps their chicks had hatched; perhaps they had not. The females could not know.

Meanwhile the male penguins had nursed the eggs, keeping them from the numbing cold. When blizzards roared with cutting winds and driving snow, they drew closer together, sharing warmth. Living on the fish and squid which they had caught in the autumn, they had grown thinner and thinner. Now they knew it was time for the females to return.

Across the icy ridges, they saw black heads bobbing and heard voices rising up, riding on the wind. They called back, trumpeting a welcome.

23

The female penguin called to her mate, and he called back. They called and called to each other. Through the hubbub of trumpeting, the female recognised her mate's voice and headed straight towards him. They greeted each other.

Their chick had not hatched yet, but there were many chicks nearby. The male passed the egg to the female, who quickly tucked it away.

Now it was the male penguin's turn for the long, long trek to the open sea. He set off and trudged with the other males, while the females cared for the newly-hatched chicks and the remaining eggs.

The chick had grown and changed and grown within the egg. Now it was ready. The egg was a prison. The chick struggled: it needed room; it needed air; it wanted to be free. With a kick and a heave it lifted its legs and wings and cracked the shell.

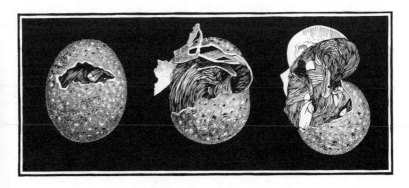

After a few moments it heaved and kicked again, and the crack grew wider.

Out came a young male chick and opened his eyes. The wind caught him suddenly and he fell over, but his mother's nudging beak set him upright.

At the same moment, she welcomed him with her voice into the Antarctic world. This was the first sound he heard, and he would never forget it. There were other voices, too — thousands of voices all around. But he heard and knew the special sound of his mother's voice. Instinctively he knew that, by keeping close to her, he would be safe.

# Penguin Film

Karen and Greg stood again on the ice overlooking the rookery. They filmed the arrival of the females. That night Greg sent another fax to his family.

| | |
|---|---|
| DATE: | **23 October 1990** |
| FAX TO: | **Sue and Peta, 61 8 8234 1234** |
| FROM: | **Dad, Mawson Base, Antarctica** |
| No. OF PAGES: | **1** |
| SUBJECT: | **Another fax to my darling daughters** |

*Dear Sue and Peta,*
*Your turn for a fax. Thank you very much for your lovely letters and drawings. I have pinned them all up by my bed — a gallery!*

*Filming was exciting today. The females returned after  months away fishing. Each heard her mate call and waddled straight up to him. How they can hear each other when all the others are racketing on, I don't know!*

*Some of the eggs have hatched. Others will hatch in the next few days. Now it is the males' turn to go fishing.*

*I can't wait to see you! How much have you grown? How heavy is Harry? I'm looking forward to seeing all the photos.*

*Much love to you all,     DAD*

The next day, they filmed the males' departure. Then, on the outskirts of the rookery, they chose a female with an egg and set up the camera. When it was time, they filmed in close-up the hatching of the downy, grey chick and its watching mother — and they tape-recorded their voices.

# Harry's Growing Fast

Meanwhile, back at Greg's home, it was Harry's bathtime. He specially liked bathtime at the weekends when Sue and Peta helped and talked to him.

'Daddy's coming home soon,' said Sue. 'You know, he's a scientist with a team from the Conservation Foundation filming in the Antarctic . . .'

Peta interrupted. 'You see, Harry, although Antarctica is a frozen desert, it's got lots of birds.'

'And huge fishing grounds all around with seals and whales, too.'

'It's got oil and minerals deep underground . . .'

'And some companies are planning to mine it . . .'

'What happens to the wildlife if they do?'

'If a fishing company takes a lot of fish there won't be enough food for the seals.'

'What if they mine where there's a penguin rookery?'

'Get your camera, Sue,' said Jan. 'Take another set of photos for Daddy. Harry's growing fast.'

They took photos of Harry by himself, Harry with the girls, and Harry with his mother. He gurgled, enjoying his bath and the voices of his mother and sisters.

'Let's make a tape,' said Sue. 'Sing, Mum!'

So Jan wrapped Harry in a towel and jigged him on her knee, singing "Dance to your Daddy". Harry gurgled and laughed, and Sue recorded his voice on tape.

'We ought to tape him in the evenings,

too,' said Peta, tickling Harry. 'Let Daddy know what it's like when he shrieks and howls and won't stop.'

'In two months time, Daddy'll be home,' said Peta. 'We ought to show him what a nuisance Harry is.'

And Harry laughed.

# Penguin Family

The emperor penguin chick grew fast, feeding on fish and squid from the female's stomach. At first he stayed close to her body and her voice.

His whole world was the rookery, filled with chicks and female penguins.

Meanwhile, his father reached the shore and, with the other males, began to feed. In three weeks their stomachs were full of fish and squid, and they returned.

As they crossed the stony ridges near the rookery, they trumpeted to the females and the chicks. The females answered. The chorus of calling grew louder, closer, and the answering chorus grew urgent.

The chicks called with their mothers and, for the first time, heard the voices of their fathers. The male penguins heard the new voices of their chicks. They hurried on, straight to the place where they waited.

At last  the rookery was filled with penguin families.

But now it was the female penguins' turn to leave and  gather food, while the males cared for the chicks.  The females set off once more.

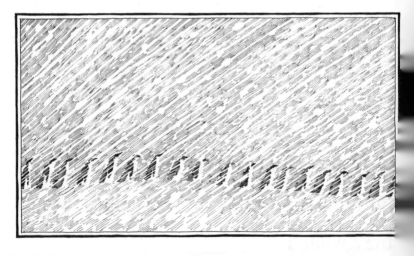

Soon the chicks became adventurous, daring to move away from their fathers, and playing with each other — jabbing with their beaks, slapping with their flippers, quarrelling and jostling.

They were growing up.

# Harry's Family

Greg showed the films he and Karen had shot, and switched off the projector.

'The penguin chick will be growing fast now,' he said. 'Soon he'll lose his downy coat. Underneath are water-proof feathers. He'll be playing with the other chicks.'

'Sometimes several parents will go off fishing,' said Karen. 'One adult will look after all their chicks. Spring is coming and the ice is breaking up, so the feeding journeys will get shorter.'

'When that chick is ready to learn to fish for himself, the ocean will be at his feet.'

Harry listened to the unfamiliar voices, and stared at his father.

'Come, little Harry,' said Greg, picking him up and jigging him on his knee. 'I'm your Dad! You'll know me soon.'

'Sue, show Dad the photos you took,' said Jan.

'I'll get the tapes,' said Peta. Greg looked at them all, and compared the pictures of Harry as a new-born baby with his appearance now.

'How you've grown while I've been away,' he said. 'Before too long you'll be able to talk.'

Harry began to know his father. He recognised Greg's voice and squealed with joy when he came home from work.

Soon Harry was eating solid food — sometimes it was mashed up fish!

Meanwhile, Greg and Karen and the conservation team were very busy producing the films about the life-cycle of the emperor penguins and the fragility of their habitat. These would be shown all around the world.

## Survival

While he was growing up, the emperor penguin chick learnt to use his voice more loudly, trumpeting to communicate, trumpeting for safety and survival.

Gradually the ice melted, and by the time the great ocean was at his feet, he was ready to fish for himself.

Like a torpedo, the young penguin dived for squid, and a hungry leopard seal lunged at him. The penguin dodged the lightning snap of jaws, rocketed out of the water and soared dolphin-like through the air. Snatching a breath, he dived back and propelled himself fast towards the bank. He leapt out, landed feet first on a ledge and trumpeted in triumph.

Safe!

# OTHER BOOKS BY EDEL WIGNELL

*Amanda's Warts*
*Battlers of the Great*
  *Depression*
*Big April Fools*
*A Bluey of Swaggies*
*A Boggle of Bunyips*
*A Bogy Will Get You!*
*Born to Lead*
*The Car Wash Monster*
*Carrying the Swag*
*Crutches Are Nothing:*
  *A Collection of Twelve*
  *Stories About Disabled*
  *Children*
*Escape by Deluge*
*Fiorella's Cameo*
*Ghost Dog*
*The Ghostly Jigsaw*
*A Gift of Squares*
*The Little Girl and*
  *her Beetle*

*Marmalade, Jet and*
  *the Finnies*
*Mischief Makers*
*Missing*
*The Nursery Rhyme Picnic*
*No Pets allowed*
*Omar's Opal Magic*
*The Portland Fairy Penguins*
*Raining Cats and Dogs*
*Rick's Magic*
*Roly Meets the Monster*
*Saving Wildlife*
*She'll Fall In, For Sure!*
*Spider in the Toilet*
*Swagmen and Sundowners*
*The Tie Olympics*
*Tucker*
*Voices*
*What's in the Red Bag?*
*What's Your Hobby?*
*You'll Turn Into a Rabbit!*

# OTHER BOOKS BY DAVID KENNETT

*Anansi & the Rubber Man*
*Baleen*
*Changing Shape*
*Folktales — a short anthology*
*Herbertia the Vile*
*Huggly Snuggly Pets*
*Jennifer and Nicholas*
*Lucky I Have My Umbrella*

*The King's Gift*
*Little Burnt-Face*
*Patrick*
*The Sea of Gold*
*The Tiger, The Brahmin &*
  *The Jackal*
*Two Feet*
*Voices*

# THE JUNIOR NOVELS BIG BOOKS